Edward Albee's

Occupant

A SAMUEL FRENCH ACTING EDITION

FOUNDED 1830

NEW YORK HOLLYWOOD LONDON TORONTO

SAMUELFRENCH.COM

ISBN 978-0-573-66380-2   Printed in U.S.A.   #7748

IMPORTANT BILLING AND CREDIT REQUIREMENTS

All producers of *EDWARD ALBEE'S OCCUPANT must* give credit to the Author of the Play in all programs distributed in connection with performances of the Play, and in all instances in which the title of the Play appears for the purposes of advertising, publicizing or otherwise exploiting the Play and/or a production. The name of the Author *must* appear in conjuction with the title of the play on a separate line on which no other name appears, immediately above the title and *must* appear in size of type not less than one hundred percent of the size of the title type. The title should read:

EDWARD ALBEE'S
OCCUPANT

In addition, the following billing must appear in all programs associated with the Play:

"EDWARD ALBEE'S
OCCUPANT

**"World Premiere originally produced
by Signature Theatre Company, New York City
James Houghton, Founding Artistic Director
Erika Mallin, Executive Director"**

In addition, all licenses issued by the Agent for production of the Play hereunder shall include the following cautionary note:

**"Licensee is not authorized to reproduce any works by Louise
Nevelson in connection with the production, advertising, and/or
promotion of the Play."**

EDWARD ALBEE'S OCCUPANT was first produced by the Signature Theater Company, (James Houghton, Founding Artistic Director; Erika Mallin, Executive Director) at the Peter Norton Space in New York City on June 5, 2008. The performance was directed by Pam MacKinnon, with sets by Christine Jones, costumes by Jane Greenwood, lighting by David Lander, and makeup by Angelina Avallone. The Production Stage Manager was Lloyd Davis Jr. The cast was as follows:

NEVELSON .... Mercedes Ruehl

THE MAN .... Larry Bryggman

THE CHARACTERS

NEVELSON – Much like the later photographs.
The **MAN** – 40s; pleasant.

THE SET

Two or three platforms stretching across the stage. Ultimately Nevelson's sculpture will fill edges, how and when to be determined. Very little else; maybe a bench.

ACT ONE

(MAN comes on stage.)

MAN. Good evening *(or "good day")* Ladies and Gentlemen...*(indicating)*...the great American sculptor... Louise Nevelson.

(NEVELSON enters, to applause.)

NEVELSON. *(improvising)* Thank you; thank you; thank you, etc. *(sees MAN is behaving oddly)* You're nervous dear?

MAN. A little bit. I've never interviewed someone who is dead before.

NEVELSON. Yeah? Well, I haven't been interviewed since I'm dead. So...we're both nervous. We'll get through it. *(indicates)* Go on.

MAN. Louise Nevelson was born in...

NEVELSON. Wait; wait. People don't know who I am?

MAN. Hm?

NEVELSON. You have to introduce me? People don't know who I am? They look at me and they don't say, 'Look, that's Louise Nevelson'?

MAN. Some; probably.

NEVELSON. Some! Look, dear, everybody knows who I am; everybody...

MAN. *Did*, maybe. Time passes. You're not as...recognizable now as you were.

NEVELSON. You're kidding!

MAN. No; time *passes.*

NEVELSON. *(arguing)* People who know about art, who know about sculpture...

MAN. Yes! People who *knew* you *know* you.

NEVELSON. Everybody...

MAN. …who knows who you *were* knows who you *are.* I mean…who do you think you are? No offence.

NEVELSON. No, of course not. None taken. Is that what they say…none taken?

MAN. Yes, sometimes. I mean, people go to a museum, they look at your work, maybe, and maybe they know it's by you, but how many people go to museums? God, half the people in this country don't know who their *senators* are much less who does the sculpture they…

NEVELSON. All right! Nobody knows who I am! Fine! Let it alone!

MAN. *(placating)* Everybody knows who you are if they know anything, but I bet I could go right outside and ask the first twenty people walking by, "Pardon me, who is Louise Nevelson?"

NEVELSON. All right!

MAN. …and maybe one will have heard of you. And try the wheat fields of Kansas, or wherever.

NEVELSON. I said…all right!

MAN. So: anybody who *knew* you *knows* you – and they know everybody else, too. They know Henry Moore, and Calder, and Stella, and Bourgeois…

NEVELSON. *(feigned)* Who?

MAN. Bourgeois; Louise Bourgeois.

NEVELSON. *(beat)* Never heard of her. *(out)* Who is *she?*

MAN. *(laughs)* Now, now! *(previous tone)* The people who know you know you. And I bet even then a lot more know what you look like than what you do – did. *(points to photo, which we see)* They know *that* a lot more than they know your work.

NEVELSON. *(in)* All right! So I'm invisible! Or I don't exist! Which do you want?

MAN. *(sighs)* I just want to tell a few things.

NEVELSON. *(shrugs)* So…go ahead. *(indicates audience) Tell* them.

MAN. *(mildly put out)* Thank you.

NEVELSON. *(disbelief)* More people know my picture than what I do...what I did?

MAN. You're a very famous image, Louise...you were. Time passes, you know.

NEVELSON. *Tell* me! What is it now? *(She refers to present year.)*

MAN. Two thousand and nine *(or whatever it is at performance)*

NEVELSON. Shit! I'm dead twenty-one *(or whatever is correct)* years now and nobody knows who I am?

MAN. That's not what I said. What I said was...

NEVELSON. *(impatient)* I know, I know, I know. I heard you. Nobody knows anything about anything except maybe one or two people. You might as well not exist – have existed...

MAN. *(gently needling)* Well, sure, if fame is the only thing that matters.

NEVELSON. Fuck you.

MAN. *(amused)* Now, now.

NEVELSON. Not fame – recognition of what you've done that matters.

MAN. O.K. *(out)* Louise Nevelson...great American sculptor. *(in)* All right?

NEVELSON. *(shrugs)* Sure.

MAN. I mean...

NEVELSON. *(speculating)* Louise Nevelson. Yes, of course. What was the rest?

MAN. Great American Sculptor.

NEVELSON. Great? Well, you said it; I didn't.

MAN. What *is* this...false modesty?

NEVELSON. *(pique)* I said you said it! *I* know who I am; *I* know how good my stuff is...but you never heard me call myself great. What I *think* – what I *know* – and what I *say* about what I *think* – what I *know*...

MAN. All right! All right!

NEVELSON. There was a long time people said what I did was crap.

MAN. I know.

NEVELSON. So, I kept on doing it and finally they came around – some of them did, most of them; maybe not the Berg boys...

MAN. *(out)* The Berg boys – Greenberg and Rosenberg. Clement Greenberg and Harold Rosenberg, the two most important art critics in town. Tastemakers; dictators.

NEVELSON. Right; not those two, but most of them came around – eventually. They came around, but *I* never said it in public: "I am the great Louise Nevelson." No matter *what* I thought.

MAN. *(laughs) (in)* O.K! O.K! Any arguments? Is "great" O.K.?

NEVELSON. *(shrugs)* Naaaaaah; it's O.K. What was the rest... American? American sculptor? American? Sure, when I was what – twenty, twenty-one? I was Russian.

MAN. No, no; you were American; you came over when you were six, and so...

NEVELSON. Four and a half.

MAN. Six. Six, to be exact.

NEVELSON. Four and a half!

MAN. No.

NEVELSON. You'd think I'd know.

MAN. Yes; one would. You were six.

NEVELSON. *(grudging)* Soooooo...maybe I was six, but I didn't become a citizen until...

MAN. *(heavy sigh)* ...until you got married. O.K.!

NEVELSON. I was born in Russia!

MAN. ...and you came over here when you were six! You're American!

NEVELSON. I was born in Kiev.

MAN. No, you weren't.

NEVELSON. No?

MAN. No: Jews weren't allowed in Kiev. You were born *near* Kiev.

NEVELSON. So?

MAN. So.

NEVELSON. So, I was Russian – for all the good it did.

MAN. Let's drop it.

NEVELSON. O.K.

MAN. Do facts *mean* anything to you?

NEVELSON. *(shrugs)* They can be useful. *(out)* No?

MAN. Anyway…sculptor: great American sculptor? Is that O.K.? Sculptor?

NEVELSON. *(in)* What else! Of course: sculptor. What else is there?

MAN. *(settling it)* Louise Nevelson – great American sculptor.

NEVELSON. Fine; good. Great American sculptor. Good. *(pause)* You know, dear, if you're born someplace and you don't feel *right* there…

MAN. *(helping)* …Near Kiev? Jewish? Pogroms?

NEVELSON. Whatever. And you come over here…

MAN. Rockland, Maine…

NEVELSON. …whatever, and you don't feel right there either, and you move to New York City when you get married, and you don't feel right there *either* – with *anything* – what do you do? *(out)* What do you *do?* You don't fit in – so you make everything fit to you. That's what you do. *(in)* That's what you do.

MAN. Yes.

NEVELSON. That's what you do.

MAN. I know. *(out)* Leah Berliawsky – shtetl, near Kiev, 1899. Father Isaac, Mother Minna Zeisel Smolerank.

NEVELSON. *(to herself, primarily)* What a marvelous name Minna Zeisel Smolerank. She didn't want to marry him, you know – my mother. He scared her; he was older; she was fifteen.

MAN. Sixteen.

NEVELSON. Whatever! Whatever makes the most sense.

MAN. The best story?

NEVELSON. *(out)* Ignore him. He scared her; he pursued her she couldn't get away from him. So…she married him.

MAN. *(in)* What a nice story.

NEVELSON. Thank you.

MAN. You want us to believe it?

NEVELSON. *(shrugs)* Suit yourself.

MAN. I bet she liked him…good-looking guy. I bet she wanted to marry him all along.

NEVELSON. *(in)* Don't be too sure. We don't always do what we do because we know what we're doing. Or we do know what we're doing but it's for other reasons.

MAN. *(broad)* Could you possibly be talking about your *own* marriage?

NEVELSON. If the shoe fits…*(afterthought)* Wait, if the shoe fits you should probably get a larger size – or a smaller one. I don't remember.

MAN. Whichever.

NEVELSON. Whichever. *(out)* Which is it? – smaller? larger?

MAN. The saying is…if the shoe fits, wear it.

NEVELSON. *(pause; suspicious)* What are you *after*?

MAN. Hm?

NEVELSON. What are you…doing?

MAN. I don't…

NEVELSON. You're after something.

MAN. *(genuine)* You. I'm after you.

NEVELSON. *(smiles)* Yeah? Who's *that*? Who am *I*? I'm a lot of people, honey and I shift all the time. You got a tough row to hoe, Mister. Is that the expression?

MAN. Yes.

NEVELSON. And what does it mean? What tough row?

MAN. You're vamping.

NEVELSON. I'm what?

MAN. You're avoiding me.

NEVELSON. Maybe I don't like what you're doing – what you're after.

MAN. You're so…*(dismissive gesture)* never mind. *(new attack)* Russian! You say you're Russian!? You never even *spoke* Russian!

NEVELSON. We spoke Yiddish.

MAN. Yes!

NEVELSON. *(not too pleasant)* We were Jews; we lived in a shtetl! It was Russia; we were Jews!

MAN. Yes, and so everybody kept leaving – everybody who could! Your father, his brothers…

NEVELSON. Of course! America, the land of…whatever… We spoke Yiddish; we were Jews. We couldn't even own land in Russia. Why would we speak Russian?

MAN. *(a little dubious)* And it was better in *Maine*, in Rockland, *Maine*? Down into Maine from Canada? Your father – him and his brothers? Why not New York?

NEVELSON. Anywhere, probably; anywhere you could get. He sent money for us, finally – for my mother and the rest of us; he saved up; he sent us passage.

MAN. Is it true that when he left you all to go to America you were so upset you wouldn't speak at all for over a year?

NEVELSON. Where did you hear that!? Maybe; maybe not. Couldn't, not wouldn't; I was abandoned.

MAN. With your whole family around you?…Your mother, your sister, your brother? You say you were…

NEVELSON. He left! He left us! He was the one I talked to!

MAN. Yes? Really? You missed him that much, eh? You, three years old, or four, or whatever?

NEVELSON. Well…something. I am a very shy woman, you know. *(out)* I am; I'm very shy.

MAN. *(scoffing)* Yeah; sure.

NEVELSON. *(quiet)* You don't know anything. *(out)* He doesn't know anything.

MAN. *(hand up, in surrender)* All right; you're very shy. So you got to Maine…

NEVELSON. So we got to Maine, and there were maybe three families – all Jews, and the rest were – what did they call them? – Yankees?

MAN. Yes: Yankees. More persecution.

NEVELSON. Hm? Well, yeah; some; a little *(out)* I mean, you live all huddled together; you don't speak English; You feel strange; maybe that makes you a stranger – you feel like one. But you go on, and you – what is the word? – you assimilate. You try to assimilate. You learn English; you go to school; you huddle together, but you reach out.

MAN. To the Yankees? You reach out to the Yankees?

NEVELSON. *(in)* To whatever's out there. You know you'll never fit in; you know you'll always be a...an exotic, is that the word? – but you go ahead as if you didn't know that. You get ahead. You help your parents and you get ahead.

MAN. Your father makes out pretty well – furniture and stuff. What's the joke...we buy junk; we sell antiques?

NEVELSON. *(sour)* Yes? Is that the joke? I don't know.

MAN. And he buys land...

NEVELSON. *(more enthusiastic)* Yes! He bought land. Just think of that! A Jew could buy land in Rockland, Maine. He worked himself up.

MAN. And on top of that...

NEVELSON. *(angry)* Why do we have to go through all this!? We were poor; we were cold; we didn't have glass in the windows! We pulled ourselves up. My father made the most of it – the most of everything. He worked his ass off. He threw me in the ocean to make me swim! He was like that – whatever he *did* he *did.* We assimilated. Nachman became Nathan, Chaya became Anita, and I became Louise.

MAN. Leah to Louise.

NEVELSON. But we never changed our last name! Berliawsky; that stayed! What were we supposed to become – Berkley, or something? No! We were proud! My mother dressed us up when we went out walking, or to school, whenever we went out. She put me in wonderful clothes; she found them; she made them. I loved them. People would stare at me as I walked to school: who's that princess? I was regal, and I was extravagant. So, my mother was a little crazy the way she got us up but, by God, people knew we were there!

MAN. Which has something to do with the way you dress now?

NEVELSON. What! You think I dress funny? I dress like *me*. I always *did*; I always *have*.

MAN. *(apologetic)* I know; I know.

NEVELSON. People look at us; they see what we show them. I dress like *me*, so that's what they see – *me*.

MAN. You're how you dress?

NEVELSON. I'm the total of everything I do.

MAN. *(to pin it down)* You dress to be noticed.

NEVELSON. *(sarcasm)* No; I dress to be invisible! Of course I dress to be noticed. I expect people to *look* at me – at me and what I *do!*

MAN. They're the same thing?

NEVELSON. *(out)* Who is this guy!? You understand, no? *(in)* They understand.

MAN. Yes, I do, too. I want to be sure you do.

NEVELSON. *(instead of replying)* I gotta go pee. *(exits)*

MAN. It's just that…*(watching her go)* It's just that she's a very complicated woman. What's the old joke…true if interesting? And what did Blanche Dubois in *Streetcar* say…I tell what ought to be true? Or is it she forgets? Or maybe she doesn't care? I think it's a little bit of each, and maybe true isn't what we're after, or maybe true is what applies. As I say, she's a very complicated woman. But…life is pretty complicated, too. You know, there's a lot written about her. There were a lot of stories and interviews stretching over a long time, and things shifted: a lot of contradictions, a lot of evasions, a lot of…careful misrememberings, a lot of scores being settled, and a lot of…well…outright lies.

NEVELSON. *(re-entering)* I heard that.

MAN. *(mouth open in astonishment)* You weren't peeing at all.

NEVELSON. No?

MAN. No, you were listening!

NEVELSON. So?

MAN. How much did you hear?

NEVELSON. Enough; some.

MAN. Sorry.

NEVELSON. A lot of outright *lies?*

MAN. Well....

NEVELSON. Listen, dear; tell me something...who *am* I?

MAN. Hm?

NEVELSON. What was my name...when I was born?

MAN. Leah Berliawsky.

NEVELSON. And...?

MAN. ...and you became Louise Nevelson.

NEVELSON. *(nods)* O.K. with any luck you turn into whoever you want to *be,* and with even *better* luck you turn into whoever you *should* be. No, you got somebody in you right from the start, and if you're lucky you figure out who it is and you *become* it. People who don't *become* are... well, look around you. So, don't talk to me about facts.

MAN. But there are *facts,* and...

NEVELSON. ...and *most* of them are *O.K.*

MAN. Oh. So...you always knew you were going to become Louise Nevelson.

NEVELSON. Don't be stupid! I knew I was going to become somebody very special. No...that I *was* somebody very special.

MAN. But you didn't know then that...

NEVELSON. ...but I had no idea what it *was* – what the special *was* – just that it *was.* I had to grow into it, I guess. If I'd known when I was a little girl that one day...

MAN. But you started drawing! You were just a kid!

NEVELSON. *(derisive wave)* Nyyaah! All kids draw; all kids are creative – naturally – even the dumb ones.

MAN. But you've bragged about how you started drawing
when you...

NEVELSON. Bragged!?

MAN. Mentioned; talked about it.

NEVELSON. I did hunh? *(shrugs)* So? Maybe I did.

MAN. And...so...?

NEVELSON. And so nothing. What did I know? That was a
long time ago. I took piano lessons, too. I took singing
lessons. *(a sudden remembrance)* Oh! Did I ever tell you
that when I was a little baby – maybe a month old – the
great Sholom Aleichem – his sister lived next to my
parents – he came to see us. And... *(indicates audience)*
Does anybody here know who he is, who he was?

MAN. *(out)* Great Yiddish writer; Russian. *(in)* Yes, I think
so.

NEVELSON. He came to visit, this was in Russia, and he took
me up in his hands and he said to my family that I was
destined for greatness – a baby; a little baby.

MAN. Built for greatness was the way I heard it. Built.

NEVELSON. Built? Destined? So?

MAN. There's a difference, maybe.

NEVELSON. *(cool)* Translation, probably *(effusive; gesturing)*
The great Sholom Aleichem, holding me aloft! "Des-
tined for greatness."

MAN. *(shakes his head; grudgingly)* That's pretty impressive.

NEVELSON. You're damn right.

MAN. *(slight smile)* True if interesting?

NEVELSON. *(sharp)* What!?

MAN. Nothing. When did you decide?

NEVELSON. What?

MAN. That you were an artist.

NEVELSON. I don't think that way.

MAN. Oh, come on!

NEVELSON. I don't!

MAN. One of your biographies says when you were nine
you knew...

NEVELSON. *(dismissive)* Oh, that! That we kids were in the library and some librarian or teacher or something asked us what we wanted to be when we grew up and I suddenly said 'I'm going to be a sculptor'? And it frightened me and I started crying and ran home? That one?

MAN. *(smiles)* Yeah; that one.

NEVELSON. I wonder if that happened, or I dreamed it? I mean I always knew I was different, that I was…special, but special doesn't always mean happy, or talented or…or whatever. Special can be one eye in the center of your forehead.

MAN. Cyclops.

NEVELSON. Hm? What? Special is…special, and I always knew that.

MAN. *(holds up invisible baby)* "Destined for greatness."

NEVELSON. Yeah, but with two eyes and two ears and one mouth and all the rest; normal, except…different. And let me tell you, there wasn't much time to figure it all out. We were poor, and we had to raise ourselves!

MAN. Yeah, and your family did pretty well.

NEVELSON. My father worked his ass off, and we all helped, and…

MAN. …and by the time you were fifteen he owned half of Rockland.

NEVELSON. *(laughs)* Not quite. Fifty-one parcels of property. Fifty-one! Isn't that something? The immigrant Jew from the Ukraine?

MAN. Pretty impressive. Is there any truth to the story your father wanted to buy a fine house for you all to live in, and you went with him to look at it, and you were sixteen, maybe, and you told him it was too fine? That it embarrassed you?

NEVELSON. *(thinks)* Maybe; vaguely. That it was wrong – for us, probably; for me. It was…oppressive? Overwhelming? I've never wanted anything to *own* me – or *any*one. I've never wanted to *belong* to anything – or any*one*, I guess.

MAN. …which brings us to the subject of your marriage, I would imagine.

NEVELSON. So soon?

MAN. Yes.

NEVELSON. *(sad)* So soon.

MAN. Do you want to tell it, or shall I?

NEVELSON. You can start…

MAN. And if what I know doesn't jibe with…

NEVELSON. Just get on with it.

MAN. O.K.

NEVELSON. If I don't like the way it's going I'll fix it ..

MAN. I bet you will. *(small pause)* OK. So. You turned into a real beautiful young lady, didn't you.

NEVELSON. *(factual)* Unh-hunh.

MAN. …tall, great figure, great face…

NEVELSON. Unh-hunh. Yep, for all the good it did. I was still a Jew from Russia. You think the other girls at school had me to their parties? Not on your life!

MAN. It was probably their parents.

NEVELSON. Maybe, but I didn't have many friends. *(chuckles)* Here's a funny story! I was tall, as you say, and not bad looking, and my skin wasn't that pasty white so many of the girls had – what you could see through the acne – it was darker, and clear, and…healthy-looking. And, one day, one of the mothers was walking her daughter to school came up to me and ran her thumb over my cheek – to see if I had makeup on! But I didn't; it was just me…healthy-looking and…different…They didn't want me around. I was invited to one party once – they had to – it was at some home, for the basketball team, and I was captain because I was so tall, and I got so nervous – being invited – that I pee'd in my pants right there.

MAN. Jesus! Did you date…at all?

NEVELSON. *(scoffing)* Hanh! Are you kidding? One of the boys at school – he was a basketball player; so was I, remember? I was tall, and athletic? – the teacher at school, the coach, maybe, told him to take me to something – a prom? I don't remember – and he said, "I don't want to take that Jew," and he wouldn't. (**MAN** *shakes his head.*) So; no, it wasn't too happy a time. I mean, I had my family, my sisters, and my brother and…

MAN. The nest.

NEVELSON. Yeah; the nest.

MAN. *(casual)* But sooner or later birds leave the nest? Or get pushed out?

NEVELSON. Sure. Plus – didn't I tell you this? – feeling special and all I was…impatient, I guess. There was a big world out there; so why was I doing all the stuff I was doing – the art lessons, the singing lessons, the piano lessons – and I was good at all of them…very good… all the – what is it called? – the extracurricular stuff ever since I was little, if it wasn't supposed to…turn into something. *Mean* something.

MAN. Lots of kids do art and stuff, but it doesn't do anything to their lives.

NEVELSON. Sure, but it doesn't make everyone feel…that *special,* as special as *I* did.

MAN. "Destined for greatness."

NEVELSON. Something! I guess I knew I had to…move on.

MAN. And away.

NEVELSON. *(defensive)* I loved my family!

MAN. Sure.

NEVELSON. I mean, my mother was sick a lot – disturbed, you know? – but we all loved each other. My father scared me a little, but we all loved each other. We'd been through so much.

MAN. But there was moving on to do.

NEVELSON. *(definition)* There was getting to where you were supposed to be – wherever that was.

MAN. There was moving *on*…and there was moving *up.*

NEVELSON. What?

MAN. *Up.* Moving *up.*

NEVELSON. Well, yeah; sure. You better yourself.

MAN. I've read that not all marriages in the old world, as they call it, that not all marriages were based entirely on love.

NEVELSON. *(noncommittal)* Oh?

MAN. Yeah, that sometimes sons and daughters married as a kind of moving up in the world.

NEVELSON. *(ibid)* Yeah?

MAN. Yeah, that a lot of marriages were – how shall I put it? – business arrangements.

NEVELSON. *(ibid)* Yeah; I've heard that.

MAN. So; so, Miss Berliawsky, tell me about the Nevelson family.

NEVELSON. Don't be funny.

MAN. *(smiles)* Sorry. So, *tell* me about them; tell me about all of *that.*

NEVELSON. "All of that"?

MAN. Engagement; leaving home; marriage; a son; disenchantment.

NEVELSON. I don't want to talk about it.

MAN. Yes, but…

NEVELSON. I said, I don't want to talk about it! It's too important.

MAN. You have to!

NEVELSON. "I have to"!? *(out)* Did you hear this? I have to talk about it?

MAN. *(consults notes)* Let me see; you were nineteen, I think.

NEVELSON. *(out)* Pay no attention to him.

MAN. *(out; notes)* In nineteen seventeen Louise Berliawsky met Bernard Nevelson, a Lithuanian Jew, born in Latvia, in eighteen…

NEVELSON. *(in; angry)* All right! I'll *tell* it! *I'll* tell it. *I'll* do it. What are we going to do – talk about everything? Every fucking thing!?

MAN. *(shrugs)* Only what matters.

NEVELSON. Everything matters!

MAN. And so…

NEVELSON. *(softer)* Let me do it.

MAN. Do it.

NEVELSON. *(quiet)* All right. *(out)* I'll tell it my way…so you'll understand. I'd finished school, and I was doing some – what do they call it? – *temp* work at an office – a lawyer's office.

MAN. *(out; an aside)* Legal stenographer. *(sotto voce)* She actually managed to graduate from school.

NEVELSON. *(to MAN)* Shut up!

MAN. *(false)* Sorry.

NEVELSON. Jesus! *(out)* Legal stenographer; all right, but temp work, just to keep busy, to bring in a little money – for myself. And one day, a man walked into the office – a client, probably. *(in)* A client?

MAN. Oh, I'm allowed to talk?

NEVELSON. Forget it. *(out)* This man walked in – fifty maybe; tall; thin; a little balding, and for some reason I knew he was a Jew; I knew he wasn't from "around"; and he walked in, and I spoke to him in Yiddish, right away, just like that! In Yiddish! And I was right; he was a Jew, a Lithuanian Jew, and was in the shipping business – he had ships. I don't know why I knew he was Jewish, but I *know* things. I have insights and I trust them. I liked this man; I was shy but I felt O.K. with him. He was – what? – fifty? There was a kind of…electricity?… between us? I liked him. He invited me to have dinner with him that night, at the hotel he was staying at…*(in)* The Thorndyke, was it?

MAN. Yes.

NEVELSON. Thanks. *(out)*…along with a sea captain he had with him – for one of his ships, I think. I told you I was shy, and here was this older man – and I'd never been in a hotel in my life, and what if he pirated me away on one of his ships!

MAN. How naive *were* you!?

NEVELSON. *(in; hard)* Very!

MAN. How did your family feel about this – you going to dinner. You *told* them.

NEVELSON. *(in)* I'm telling it! *(out)* They seemed to think it was O.K. He was older; he was a businessman. *(in)* I think they checked with the lawyer – where I was… whatever.

MAN. *(out)* Pretty quick work.

NEVELSON. *(in; sharp)* What!?

MAN. Go on. So what was this…your first date?

NEVELSON. It wasn't a date; it was a…social engagement.

MAN. *(smiles; out)* Oh!

NEVELSON. *(out; waving him off)* It was a social engagement, and it was nice, and the food was great – a little greasy, maybe, but good – and it was a hotel – china and mirrors – and I was all dressed up and it was wonderful… *(in)* I guess it was my first time being a grownup. He walked back home with me, and he said hello to my family. *(out)* And the next day I was told he'd left – went back to New York. And then he started writing me, writing me letters, about his family, about his brothers, about his business – his ships – about being married, and he and his wife were planning to have their first baby – that they hadn't wanted kids at first, but now they were thinking about it! He wrote me these letters, but I didn't answer them, because I was suspicious, in spite of all he said, because I'd read about those things, about robber barons having young mistresses, and so forth, and I wasn't about to get into that kind of life. So, I didn't answer his letters.

MAN. *(to* **NEVELSON***)* And maybe in part because you could barely spell. Some education!

NEVELSON. *(out)* And maybe because I was ashamed of my spelling. *(in)* YES! *(out)* So, I didn't answer his letters, but about a year after I'd had dinner and all with Bernard I got a letter from him saying his youngest

brother was coming to Rockland on business – for the
family – and would I like to meet him.

MAN. And your whole life changed.

NEVELSON. *(in)* Yes, and my whole life changed. *(out)* My
whole life changed.

MAN. *(nicely)* Tell about it.

NEVELSON. *(to herself, really)* It's very weird.

MAN. I know.

NEVELSON. *(out)* You don't know how weird. Here's what's
weird, what's so weird. When he got to Rockland – the
brother, Charles, did – he called us – on the phone! We
had one! – and said could I have dinner with him. My
mother answered; I wasn't home. I got home and my
mother told me the brother had called, and I knew…
and I knew that I would – that I would marry him.

MAN. *(out)* Charles Nevelson, thirty-seven years old, five
foot *four*? *(to* NEVELSON*)* He really looked up to you,
eh?

NEVELSON. I said, don't be funny.

MAN. *(out)* Five foot four, stocky, thirty seven years old, under
his brother's thumb. *(in)* Why *ever* did you marry him?

NEVELSON. *(in)* I don't know; I just knew I would. Sometimes you know things. It was all wanted – my family,
Bernard; I could tell that. They all wanted it, *(shrugs)*
so I guess I wanted it, too.

MAN. Oh, come on! You? Miss Free Spirit?

NEVELSON. *(in and out; uncomfortable)* I guess it was a kind
of a…a way up, a way out. I've *told* you; I'm very intui-
tive. Something comes up like that – I realize I've
already decided without knowing I'd done it. It all
came together – all the reasons – and I *knew*. I *knew* he
would ask me to marry him, and I knew I would.

MAN. Marriage at first sight. Amazing. Right there at dinner.

NEVELSON. It was that simple. *(out)* It was…that simple.

MAN. *(not pleasant) That…simple.*

NEVELSON. *(in)* Well…whatever.

MAN. *(ibid)* A way out? A way up?

NEVELSON. Sure.

MAN. *(pinning it down)* So you had dinner with him – this stranger. At the same hotel?

NEVELSON. I think so; maybe; I don't know.

MAN. *(puzzled)* And so…you had dinner with this…short, plumpish, balding man almost twice as old as you, and he asked you to marry him and you said yes.

NEVELSON. Yes.

MAN. Before dessert?

NEVELSON. *(a little dreamlike)* What? No; during.

MAN. And you said yes.

NEVELSON. Yes.

MAN. …even though it was Bernard you were attracted to.

NEVELSON. *(annoyed)* We *did* that. He was *married.*

MAN. Still, you said yes.

NEVELSON. *(fact)* Yes.

MAN. *(wanting to disbelieve)* What did you see in him – in this Charles?

NEVELSON. *(pause)* A passport, I guess. *(out; intense)* You, understand, no? A way out…up? We were immigrants; I wasn't even a citizen, and and here was this rich Nevelson family deciding I belonged with *them* – that they wanted me to be part of *their* life…in New York!

MAN. *(pause)* Well, maybe it was simple.

NEVELSON. *(in; intense)* Were you around in nineteen twenty?

MAN. No.

NEVELSON. Were you ever an immigrant?

MAN. No.

NEVELSON. Were you ever a Jew?

MAN. No.

NEVELSON. Were you ever a girl?

MAN. No; of course not.

NEVELSON. Then don't talk to me about simple. There were lots of reasons, and they all *(gestures)*…intertwined. *(out)* He doesn't *understand* anything.

MAN. *(a little sarcastic)* Right! You were suffering up there in Rockland, and…

NEVELSON. *(in)* Not suffering, for Christ's sake! It was all right, I guess, for most people, but I was…*(gently)* I was very special.

MAN. And your family probably wanted it.

NEVELSON. *(a little sad)* Sure; they wanted it.

MAN. Too?

NEVELSON. *(a beat)* Too.

MAN. And so your whole life changed.

NEVELSON. Yes; and so my whole life changed. *(long pause)* Into a pile of shit.

MAN. *(awe)* Wow!

NEVELSON. Hm?

MAN. Wow.

NEVELSON. *(apologetic)* Slowly; not at first. Why, do you find that too dramatic?

MAN. No; pretty good, but, still…wow!

NEVELSON. Thanks.

MAN. *(ironic)* Out and up, and into a pile of shit?

NEVELSON. Yeah, well. Things are seldom what they seem.

MAN. And skim milk masquerades as cream?

NEVELSON. Right; but later. We didn't get married right away. You didn't in those days. I was engaged for over a year.

MAN. I take it you two…"kept your distance?"

NEVELSON. What does that mean? *(out)* What does that mean?

MAN. I'm talking about…sex.

NEVELSON. *(in)* Well, don't!

MAN. I mean…

NEVELSON. Back in those days every girl who got married

was a virgin – went to the altar intact.

MAN. Yes, but...

NEVELSON. ...whether they were or not.

MAN. Oh, I see!

NEVELSON. *NO*, you *don't*! You *don't* see. *(pause)* All right; yes; I was. *(out)* I *was*. It was how I was raised; it was how I was brought up.

MAN. Thank you.

NEVELSON. You're welcome.

MAN. It's nice to get something cleared up.

NEVELSON. *(chuckles)* Oh, now. He brought me and my mother to New York – Charles did – and he showed us around the city. He brought us there for several weeks, and he took us everywhere, the whole family did – you know we'd never been there, my mother or me – and it was so...opening. *(out)* I mean, the great buildings, the stores, the places people lived, the concerts, the museums, the opera – and the Statue of Liberty! The water, and the sky, and this wonderful, oversized thing! It looked like she reached to heaven! *(in)* All the way to heaven.

MAN. *(smiles)* You liked it, eh? New York?

NEVELSON. It was...well, it was everything I'd *thought* it would be. It was where I belonged, and I *knew* it. *(out)* No matter what! It was where I had to be. I moved there and I lived there...forever. I saw Europe later and it was wonderful, but New York...*(shakes her head)* that was *it!* *(in)* That really was *it!*

MAN. Great. *(urging on)* And so eventually you got married.

NEVELSON. *(laughs)* In Boston, at the Coply Plaza. *(out)* Halfway between New York and Rockland. I figured everyone could go halfway. And I wore a wonderful lace dress – down to my ankles – and a huge pink hat!

MAN. You must have looked great!

NEVELSON. *(in)* Yes; I looked great. I think it was the pink hat.

MAN. Wasn't there some problem with the engagement ring?

NEVELSON. Well...in a way, yeah.

MAN. You didn't like it?

NEVELSON. *(shrugs)* It was a perfectly nice one carat diamond ring, bought at a good store.

MAN. So?

NEVELSON. So...the Nevelsons had a lot of money and I wasn't a tiny little thing. You could barely see it! I mean...big girl, big ring.

MAN. *(agreeing)* Everything in proportion.

NEVELSON. Exactly! Everything in proportion. But the big rich Nevelson family had the feeling that ostentation was vulgar, or something. Still!

MAN. Still!

NEVELSON. *(out)* And it wasn't I wanted a big ring – to show off, or whatever. I don't wear rings and stuff. It was the...principal.

MAN. Yes.

NEVELSON. *(under her breath)* Cheap little...

MAN. What!?

NEVELSON. *(in)* Ring! Cheap little *ring*. That *still* burns me up.

MAN. Tsk, tsk, tsk.

NEVELSON. Tsk, tsk, tsk. Right!

MAN. So, you *did* get married.

NEVELSON. Yeah; we got married. *(out)* We went to Havana on our honeymoon.

MAN. Tell me about it.

NEVELSON. *(in)* Havana? You want to know about Havana? Nice city, great people.

MAN. *(laughs)* No...your marriage.

NEVELSON. *(shakes her head)* You *do* want to talk about sex, don't you. *(out)* *Isn't* he something?

MAN. Well, not if you don't...

NEVELSON. *(in; imitating)* "Well, not if you don't..." Yes! You
   do! All right let's get it out of the way. *(sincere)* Sex and
   I were fine together; I want you to understand that. I
   liked sex – once I knew what it was all about. *(out)* I
   mean, sometimes I did think it was a little strange, a
   man bouncing up and down on top of you like that,
   but it was O.K., and I had my share.

MAN. I have a list of your supposed lovers.

NEVELSON. *(in)* I bet you do. *(out)* I bet he has.

MAN. *(out)* Quite a group.

NEVELSON. *(out) Listen* to him! *(in)* That list: you probably
   got people on there I never met, and some should
   be on it you don't even know about...Sex is fine; it's
   splendid, but there's stuff goes with it that no one
   should put up with.

MAN. Yes?

NEVELSON. Possession! Ownership! For sex you get possession of someone? You get to tell them what to do, how
   to live? No thank you, Sir.

MAN. And Charles tried to...tried to do *what?*

NEVELSON. When I married him he promised me a kind of
   life...We'd be married, yes. But I was supposed to go
   on with my life, with my studies, my painting lessons,
   my singing, my...

MAN. He *promised* you?

NEVELSON. Hm? Well, maybe I thought he did; maybe
   that's what I expected, so maybe I thought I'd been
   promised...

MAN. Marriage is a contract.

NEVELSON. Yeah? Maybe, but it doesn't give you...owner-
   ship. You don't own somebody just because you marry
   them. I tried to fit *in*; I tried to become all the...*stuff*
   he wanted me to be – all the social life, the parties,
   the...the...the domestic arrangements? Wife of the
   rich man, dress up, go out; be with him all the time...
   the wife *(out)* I had my own life I wanted. I wanted to

grow into *being* somebody. I didn't want to be told what I *could* do and what I couldn't – what looked proper and what didn't.

MAN. You married into a society that was...

NEVELSON. ...that wanted to approve everything I did! I tried! I played the game, but...it wasn't me.

MAN. You were expected to fit in.

NEVELSON. Yeah, to a lot of things I didn't *need*, didn't *want.*

MAN. That's life?

NEVELSON. I'd look into the mirror – the big gilt mirror in the entrance hall were we lived – on Central Park West – and I'd look at myself – all dressed to go out, fine dress, long fur coat, hair all done up, and I'd look, and I'd say "who's that!? Who's that *woman?*" I didn't recognize me.

MAN. You looked great, of course.

NEVELSON. *(in)* Well, the woman in the mirror looked great, but...who *was* she?

MAN. *(urging on)* And then...

NEVELSON. Yeah, and then I got pregnant. *(to herself; angry)* How did I *do* that!? How did I let myself *do* that!?

MAN. *(sort of a question)* Charles was the father, of course.

NEVELSON. *(in rage)* Of course Charles was the father! What do you think I *am*!?

MAN. Well, there are rumors that there were affairs.

NEVELSON. Yeah, I've heard them too – read them, but later! That was later! It was Charles and me; *me* – good, faithful wife.

MAN. It never occurred to you you'd get pregnant?

NEVELSON. I guess not.

MAN. But...

NEVELSON. It wasn't something I wanted, so I guess I thought it would never happen, or maybe I didn't think about it, or...

MAN. ...or maybe you forgot to...

NEVELSON. Drop it!

MAN. O.K.

NEVELSON. Anyway, there I was – pregnant; and I didn't want to be, and...

MAN. You didn't...

NEVELSON. What!? Try to get rid of it?

MAN. Yes.

NEVELSON. *(out)* It never occurred to me! Never!

MAN. *(calming her)* O.K.

NEVELSON. *(in)* In spite of what it did to my mother. Pregnant! Pregnant! Four of us kids. It became her whole life and look what it did to *her!*

MAN. What did it do?

NEVELSON. I don't want to get into it! *(out)* She was a good woman.

MAN. *(priming)* And so, you were going to have a baby.

NEVELSON. *(in)* Well, that was what was expected, wasn't it? Good strong girl? Strengthen the line?

MAN. I read that you insisted on a Cesarean – big healthy girl like you.

NEVELSON. Yeah. *(out)* The shrinks could have a field day with that one.

MAN. *Did* have.

NEVELSON. Right! No, I didn't want a baby, and I was a rotten mother. *(out)* But I loved him – Mike; we called him Mike: Myron, Mike.

MAN. Yeah, you were a rotten mother, weren't you.

NEVELSON. *(in)* O.K.! O.K.! All those stories!

MAN. ...how you almost let him drown at the beach – a tiny baby: you walked off and let him...

NEVELSON. I said: O.K.!

MAN. ...and how a couple of years later you almost backed over him in the *car*? He was playing and you almost backed *over* him?

NEVELSON. Yes!

MAN. And he was slow learning to speak, because you wouldn't *talk* to him?

NEVELSON. Yes! All of it! *(pause; softer)* Don't you get it? I was – what? – I was...going down, going under.

MAN. *(out)* Right, and so were the Nevelsons – the empire collapsing? – less and less money all the time? *(in)* You have to move to smaller and smaller places – to Brooklyn, finally?

NEVELSON. I was going under!

MAN. Right.

NEVELSON. *(out)* I got sick; I had to go to bed for a year!

MAN. *(like reading a list)* Depression; sciatica, abscesses, boils...

NEVELSON. *(in; rage)* My blood was boiling! *(quieter)* I was going down. *(out)* I tried – for *years*. I kept on going as best I could. I was the wife; I *tried*; I was a mother; I *tried*! But it was all...going down.

MAN. *(gentle)* Down; not...up.

NEVELSON. *(in)* Hm? Oh; right. *(out)* I guess I was having a...what do they call it?...a breakdown? A nervous breakdown? A slow...a very, very slow nervous breakdown – the walls around me? The darkness? The darkness always crowding me?

MAN. Did you think about killing yourself?

NEVELSON. *(pause; nodding; in)* Sure. Of course I did. For the first time.

MAN. Oh?

NEVELSON. There were others...later.

MAN. *(real curiosity)* What kept you from doing it?

NEVELSON. Damned if I know. *(pause; sudden awareness; to herself, mainly)* Maybe it was the horse.

MAN. The what?

NEVELSON. The horse; the big black horse.

MAN. *(confused)* I'm sorry, I don't...

NEVELSON. The horse. *(out)* I was – what? – eleven, maybe, and I was corning home from school.

MAN. In Rockland.

NEVELSON. Of course in Rockland! Where do you think? *(out)* I was coming home from school, and I was eleven maybe, and all of a sudden there was this huge black horse...running, alone, with no harness, or carriage. Maybe it'd broken away from the stable. And there it was – huge, bigger than any horse I'd ever seen. All black, and against the green everywhere – everything was in foliage, everything was in bloom – . I was running home from school, and I ran to keep up with the horse, the...huge black horse. But I couldn't, of course; so I stopped and watched as long as I could... until it vanished. I've never forgotten that. Nothing has ever affected me like that. Ever.

MAN. My goodness.

NEVELSON. It was free.

MAN. Yes.

NEVELSON. Nothing.

MAN. *(impressed)* Well.

NEVELSON. Except maybe when I was fifteen, I think. There was a neighbor who had a relative visiting – a boy. And he was known to be a good-for-nothing – the boy – He was slender, and he already looked decadent, though he must have been my age. Blue eyes; he had blue eyes. And I remember looking in his eyes and seeing depths which I've never seen again.

(pause)

MAN. My goodness *(sudden thought)* Is all this true?

NEVELSON. Hm? What?

MAN. The horse; the huge black horse: is all this true? Forget the boy. The black horse: is all this true?

NEVELSON. *(noncommittal)* Well, what do *you* think?

MAN. *(genuine; slow)* I don't know.

NEVELSON. It's interesting, isn't it.

MAN. *(sudden awareness)* True if interesting!?

NEVELSON. *(preoccupied)* Hm? What did you say?

MAN. True if interesting!? The black horse? The boy?

NEVELSON. *(genuine smile)* Oh, no; it's all true. The black horse: all true. And the boy: I never saw him again. That may be the only time I've ever been in love.

MAN. *(quite disturbed)* I think I need to…I think we should have an intermission. *(out)* We'll have an intermission.

NEVELSON. *(starting to exit)* Oh, good.

End of Act One

ACT TWO

(stage empty; **MAN** *enters)*

MAN. *(out)* Welcome back. If you're wondering why I called
an intermission back there when I did, it was…well,
very simply, I was getting confused and I wanted to
think about some things, get a little… *un*confused – a
little *less* confused than I was. I mean…look, I've heard
the story about the black horse before; I've read about
it; it's in at least two books, but in each time it's not
a quote; it's a retelling of what she *said* happened –
what she *said* the event was. It wasn't a report of what
happened; I mean, no one was *there.* Each time it was
a slightly different report of what she *said happ*ened.
It's troubling, you know? You say things enough and
people believe them. They may be *true,* but if you've
got someone you know makes things up, and admits
to it, is probably *proud* of it!…well, then, the weirdest
thing happens: what's true, what's *really* true gets a kind
of edge about it, a kind of…where's what's really *really*
true and what is embroidery, or what's just slightly mis-
remembered – no intention. The downright lies are
different; they're calculated, usually, made up for a
reason – to disprove a fact, or…make everything just
a little…ambiguous. And does this get us anywhere?
Well, maybe it does…if you like quicksand.

(NEVELSON *enters, having heard the last bit.)*

NEVELSON. You are *really somet*hing.

MAN. Every time I start talking about you, in you sneak. Do
you wait? Do you wait until I get close to the point I'm
trying to make, and then…?

NEVELSON. No, I come back in when I'm finished doing
whatever I'm doing. I was fixing my makeup.

MAN. You don't wear makeup.

NEVELSON. My eyes! My eyes! My fucking eyelashes! *(out)* I wear sable eyelashes: I wear two sets on each eye. No powder; no paint; no lipstick – in spite of what some people say – just the sable eyelashes.

MAN. Why sable?

NEVELSON. *(amazed)* Why sable!? Are you crazy!? I had a great sable coat; I had a big sable spread for my bed. *(out)* The eyes are...what? The entry to the soul? Well, I don't know about that, but they sure do call attention to themselves – the eyes – if you've got two sets of sable eyelashes on 'em.

MAN. Did you ever try three sets?

NEVELSON. *(in)* Yes; of course. I couldn't keep my eyes open. *(They both chuckle.)* Everybody thought I was asleep – standing up, walking around and talking, dead asleep.

MAN. *(to confirm)* You wore them when you worked; not just socially.

NEVELSON. *(out)* Socially? What's socially? *(in)* No...all the time. In the morning when I got up *(out)* ...*if* I got up, if I wasn't spending the day in bed, the *week* maybe.

MAN. Drinking? Is this about drinking, about the binges?

NEVELSON. *(to* **MAN***; straightforward)* What drinking? What binges? *(out)* Isn't he something? *(in)* Who the hell are you anyway? *(out)* You gotta be real careful with these types, these "interviewers." Especially if you're dead. They take all sorts of liberties. *(in)* Drank? Who Drank?

MAN. *(almost says something, doesn't; then)* I...we'll talk about it...another time...later.

NEVELSON. Talk about what? I don't know what you're talking about.

MAN. *(hands up; defeated; smiling)* O.K., O.K.

NEVELSON. *(out)* Where was I?

MAN. In the morning, when you got up, *if* you got up, if you weren't for some reason spending the *week*...

NEVELSON. *(gets it)* Oh; O.K. *(out)* What I always did was... look pretty. I never went anywhere I didn't look pretty – when I was a little girl; when I was married; all during the bad times; later. I never went anywhere I didn't look pretty. What if somebody sees you! You're going to a party…you look pretty. You're going into your studio to work; you put on your levis and…what?… a wonderful lace shawl, and a jockey's cap, maybe? Nothing special, but…pretty. You know?

MAN. And always the eyelashes.

NEVELSON. *(in)* And always the eyelashes. The focus.

MAN. And that started when?

NEVELSON. Hm? *(shrugs)* I don't know.

MAN. All that was later. I want to get back to where we were.

NEVELSON. And where was that?

MAN. The collapse of the marriage, the nervous breakdown…

NEVELSON. We did all that. *(out)* Didn't we?

MAN. I want to pick up from there.

NEVELSON. *(in)* You mean go over it all again!? *(out)* Jesus!

MAN. No; make some sense of it.

NEVELSON. *(in)* Hah! Good luck!

MAN. I want to try.

NEVELSON. *(shrugs)* Suit yourself. And what was all that stuff you were going on about the horse, and what's true, what isn't? All that stuff again?

MAN. The horse, yes.

NEVELSON. Black.

MAN. Yes; black; the black horse…

NEVELSON. I'll never forget it. *(out)* I knew I'd never catch it, I guess.

MAN. *(snorts)* Metaphor!

NEVELSON. *(in)* Hm?

MAN. You were – what? – you were eleven!? And you were thinking in metaphors!? "I knew I'd never catch it," etcetera? Is that the way you were thinking when you were eleven?

NEVELSON. *(slow smile)* I don't remember. *(out)* Do I. *(chuckles)*

MAN. *(hands up)* All right; all right! But what about the boy?

NEVELSON. *(in)* Who? What boy?

MAN. The boy; the boy when you were fifteen – the decadent boy and those eyes you looked into. Blue eyes and *(checks notes)* what did you say?...And I remember looking into his eyes and seeing scary depths which I never saw again...ever...anywhere.

NEVELSON. *(cool)* You're adding.

MAN. Still. Depths you never saw again? *(beat)* Ever?

NEVELSON. *(uncovered)* No; never. *(defensive)* I thought you didn't care about him!

MAN. No; but you did. *(beat)* Didn't you.

NEVELSON. *(slow smile)* I don't remember. *(out)* Do I. *(chuckles)*

MAN. *(gentle)* Did you love him? *(no response)* Louise?

NEVELSON. *(preoccupied)* Hm?

MAN. The boy. Did you love him?

NEVELSON. *(open)* I saw him only once. What does love have to do with it?

MAN. I don't know. What does love have to do with anything? Talk to me about love, Louise. Who did you love? Really love?

NEVELSON. *(gorge rising)* You don't know anything about anything, you and your books! Love? I loved my *family*, I love my *friends*, I...

MAN. And Mike? Did you love Mike?

NEVELSON. *(angry)* Of course I loved him! He was my son! Of course I loved him! I was a rotten mother – I told you that – and I didn't want him – not *him* – didn't not want *him* – I loved him, but I didn't want to be a mother. I didn't want to be...

MAN. Held down.

NEVELSON. *(softer)* Whatever. *(out)* He was a good boy. I don't know how he ever forgave me. I sent him off to live with the family.

MAN. In Maine.

NEVELSON. Yeah; in Maine; in Rockland. He went to good schools there. They took him back twice – his father did – came up to Rockland and persuaded my family to let them; put him in Jewish schools in New York, but he *hated* it! Both times he *hated* it! *(clearly wants to abandon the subject) (out)* He was a good boy; he grew up O.K. He was strong – like his mother.

MAN. He took up art, didn't he. He became a sculptor.

NEVELSON. *(in) (smiles)* Isn't that something!? *(out; pleased)* He did sculpture, weekends. He made structures; they were art and they were furniture. I kept one in my bedroom on Spring Street. It was wood and it looked like a...person, a...a cubist person. He was good!

MAN. *(casual)* As good as his mother?

NEVELSON. *(in)* ...what?

MAN. As good as his mother.

NEVELSON. *(pause; odd chuckle)* Don't be silly! *(pause; realizes)* Why did you make me say that!?

MAN. *(offhand)* Oh, because you have no mind of your own, because you'll say anything anyone wants you to, because you don't think before you speak, because...

NEVELSON. *(furious)* Because you tricked me! *(out)* Mike's art was good; it had integrity. Mike was a good son, a lot better than I deserved. He made a good life for himself, a good family. He was a good, steady man. And he put up with me. With *me! (in)* O.K? Can we get on to something else?

MAN. *(shrugs)* Sure.

NEVELSON. *(out)* I mean...come on!

MAN. So! You had your nervous breakdown, your...long... long nervous breakdown.

NEVELSON. *(In. Eyes narrowing)* Are you mocking me?

MAN. No, but I'm interested that you didn't make a final break with it all for ten years, and even after *that* you came back a couple of times.

NEVELSON. So?

MAN. *(smiles)* That's a really long nervous breakdown.

NEVELSON. Look; don't you know *any*thing? You have –
whatever it is – you have – call it whatever you want
– there are only two ways to handle it, this…this awful
knowledge that everything's fucked up. You go bon-
kers, or you go numb. And if you go numb you can
sleepwalk your way through it for a very long time.
People know something's wrong, but they don't know
what, and they don't know how awful the stuff inside
is…*(pokes her chest)* inside *you!* You can go on a very
long time and nobody can hear you screaming. You
know? It goes in and out, bad to very bad, very bad
back to…to what?…tolerable? Yeah; O.K.; tolerable.
Psychiatry was coming in and a friend, a good friend,
said I should do it. But I said no; *no!*; That's for *weak*
people. I'm good, tough stock. I'll get through it. And
I *did. (in)* And I *did.*

MAN. Eventually.

NEVELSON. What do you *want*!? Jesus!

MAN. Ten years!

NEVELSON. You're a good girl; you try. Sometimes you
scream so they can hear you; sometimes you do so they
can't. Ten years; yeah.

MAN. Piano lessons; singing lessons; drawing lessons; shopping lessons! The whole time!

NEVELSON. *(laughs)* Ah! You heard all about that.

MAN. *(pleased disbelief)* The worse the Nevelsons' business
troubles got, the more stuff you bought?

NEVELSON. *(pleased)* Yeah!

MAN. Crystal? Silverware? Rugs? Antiques?

NEVELSON. Yeah, and I was good at it. I had a good eye. I
only got the really good stuff.

MAN. And when it got really hairy – when you were down
to a couple of rooms in Brooklyn – you *still* went to
the fancy markets in Manhattan and had all the food
delivered!?

NEVELSON. *(reasonable)* Yeah, well...they promised me a rose garden.

(They both laugh.)

MAN. You should have gone into analysis.

NEVELSON. Naah; I knew what I wanted; I just didn't know what it was.

MAN. It might have helped.

NEVELSON. No! I learned a couple of things along the way – eventually, some later than others – and what I learned most was...you've go to do it yourself. Try to stand up, and if it turns out you can't stand up straight without crutches, go out and learn how to make crutches. Make your own.

MAN. *(applauds a little)* Very good!

NEVELSON. Thank you.

MAN. How did Charles take to all this – the lessons, the shopping, the...

NEVELSON. *(matter of fact)* We fought. All the time. "Stop shopping; you're driving me into the poorhouse! Stop ignoring Mike..."

MAN. Myron.

NEVELSON. *(in)* Yes. *(out)* "Who are you fucking!?" Believe me, it wasn't a good time.

MAN. You almost make me feel sorry for him.

NEVELSON. *(in)* Who?

MAN. Charles; the whole damn bunch of 'em.

NEVELSON. *(considers)* I guess I wasn't easy.

MAN. *(very casual)* Were you?

NEVELSON. Hm?

MAN. *Were* you? Did Charles have a point?

NEVELSON. Did the little fat bald man have a point?

MAN. You're not nice.

NEVELSON. I never claimed it. Did Charles have a point? Was I sleeping around?

MAN. Yes.

NEVELSON. *(smile)* Wouldn't you like to know.

MAN. Yes; as a matter of fact I would. None of the books about you...

NEVELSON. Well, you...you decide whatever you want. Who goes around talking about their sex lives in public!?

MAN. A lot of people.

NEVELSON. Yeah? Well, I'm not one of them. Whatever there was – if there was anything – didn't help and didn't hurt.

MAN. No boy with the blue eyes – deepest you'd ever seen, or whatever?

NEVELSON. Lay off him! No; no deep blue eyes. No nothing, probably.

MAN. And so ten years into it you finally broke off and went to Europe.

NEVELSON. Yeah, but before that I'd met somebody – the Princess Norina Matchabelli; she was Italian and she was an actress and she was married to this Russian Noble got thrown out with the revolution, and they were stuck in New York. They were broke, and so she started teaching, and I took lessons.

MAN. Was she any good?

NEVELSON. *(considers it)* Well, maybe if you wanted to act in Russian. But she did something. She taught me about some of the Eastern stuff – the philosophers, the mystics.

MAN. Oh, no!

NEVELSON. Krishnamurti and the others. *(MAN shakes his head.)* Don't make fun! What they said to me was this – the Eastern ones – "live for yourself; live *fully;* be... your*self.*" The transcendental end didn't interest me too much. "Be your*self;* be *only* yourself." The Princess introduced me to a lot of people. Frederick Kiesler was one. What a mind he had!

MAN. *(out)* Frederick Kiesler – Freiderich, actually; Austrian; architect, artist, visionary...

NEVELSON. *(out)* He took me around. He showed me art I'd never seen, never even imagined – Picasso, Klee...

MAN. His widow said you two maybe had an affair.

NEVELSON. *(in)* He was tiny! He barely came up to my *waist!*

MAN. So?

NEVELSON. *(dismissive)* Forget it! *(afterthought)* Bright man. I liked him. He knew what was going on. God knows *I* didn't.

MAN. And so you went to Europe.

NEVELSON. Yeah, I went to study with Hans Hofmann; he was the big guy then. Everybody said he was the best art teacher around. He was a pretty good artist himself.

MAN. I know.

NEVELSON. You know his work? He sort of went out of fashion after a while.

MAN. I know; but I know.

NEVELSON. I was at the Art Students League in New York. They let me in; I was good. *(out)* I mean, good for what anybody knew back then. God, nobody knew about Europe, about Picasso, about...anybody. But I heard about Hofmann, and he was teaching in Berlin...Germany, and I decided I had to go to him.

MAN. In Berlin!

NEVELSON. *(in)* Yeah.

MAN. I'm sure Charles liked that.

NEVELSON. He said no. "You're a wife; you're a mother; you stay where you belong."

MAN. In spite of everything.

NEVELSON. In spite of everything; yeah. So, I went to my family; they were doing O.K. There was money – well, not a lot, but there was money.

MAN. And they paid for your trip to Europe!?

NEVELSON. Yeah; they knew that everything was wrong. It was my mother, mostly. She understood.

MAN. Right; sure.

NEVELSON. She never had the freedom to…to do what she wanted. Not that I think she ever knew what it *was*… what she wanted. They paid for it – the trip.

MAN. So, you up and left?

NEVELSON. *(out)* Why doesn't he understand anything? What do you have to do? *(in)* I parked Mike in Maine; I told Charles I was going whether he liked it or not, and…I went.

MAN. Didn't he threaten to – what, divorce you?

NEVELSON. *(dogma)* You didn't divorce. Respectable, upper-middle-class New York Jews? Don't be dumb.

MAN. You did get divorced eventually – a lot later.

NEVELSON. *(dismisses it)* He found a woman he wanted to marry – a nice woman, probably. I never met her.

MAN. They say you did.

NEVELSON. *(shrugs)* Then maybe I did.

MAN. And so you went to Berlin.

NEVELSON. *(in)* And so I went to Berlin.

MAN. And how was Hofmann?

NEVELSON. He was a shit! The Nazis were coming and all Hofmann wanted to do was get out of Germany. He was a Jew. So the only students he paid any attention to were those he thought could help him. The rest of us he just ignored.

MAN. He also told you you had no talent, that you'd never make it as an artist.

NEVELSON. I said: he was a shit…So I left his class and I discovered Europe – the cities, the museums, the people!

MAN. You were happy.

NEVELSON. No, I wasn't happy. I was alone; I didn't know anybody; I'd been thrown out of Hofmann's art class; little Mike was writing me letters saying come home, mommy, I miss you; my money was running out! Of course I wasn't happy! *(out)* Happy, is he crazy? But every once and a while something would happen that would…what?…take me out of myself – take me beyond...*me. (out)* Like when I was back in New York and I was at the Metropolitan Museum and I walked in to a show of costumes for the Japanese Noh theatre.

MAN. *(out; ironic)* Ah, the famous Japanese robe story.

NEVELSON. *(in)* Be quiet!

MAN. *(smiles)* Sorry.

NEVELSON. *(out)* Now, let me tell you there are things in us we find parallel outside us, and it was that way with these robes. Each robe was a universe. I can tell you exactly where they were. The exhibition was on the south side of the balcony, and the manikins didn't have any heads, and I went upstairs and I looked at them – the forms – and then I looked at the material. Some of them had gold cloth with medallions, and the cloth was so finely woven that the likes of it I never saw before; and the medallion was gold, so it was gold on gold. I looked at it all, and I sat down without thinking and I had a barrel of tears in the left eye and a barrel of tears in the right eye...and then my nose was running, so there was another barrel of that, and I wanted to go to the bathroom, so there was another barrel. Everything opened up...and I knew, and I said, Oh, my God, life is worth living if a civilization can give us this. And so I sat there and wept, and wept and sat. And I went home, and it gave me a whole new life.

MAN. A whole new life?

NEVELSON. Well, a little bit of *light.* Sometimes things *happen* and they change everything and you don't know *why*...but you *do*; you *do* know why...only somewhere inside.

MAN. Moments of...revelation.

NEVELSON. Don't be pretentious. *(afterthought)* Yes; you have them; you have these. I had some. *(out)* Doesn't it happen to you, too? These...moments. Yes? No? *(They reply, or do not; improvise.)*

MAN. They *are* revelation, then.

NEVELSON. *(in)* Sure; the mystics; Picasso; the Japanese robes. There are...things.

MAN. Things...people.

NEVELSON. I knew a lot of people – later – famous people, great people, and I had the chance to meet Picasso – more than once – but I couldn't *do* it.

MAN. No?

NEVELSON. No; he was too great; he meant too much to me. There are people like that.

MAN. Were there others?

NEVELSON. I don't remember. Maybe, but not like that.

MAN. From what they tell me maybe you wouldn't have liked him.

NEVELSON. It isn't the people; it's what they *do*. I knew Celine. Did you know that?

MAN. *(astonished)* The French writer!? The Jew hater!? The Nazi!?

NEVELSON. Yes; well...you see? He had a great mind; he taught me a lot, and he wanted to marry me, but I said to him why is it you Jew haters always want to marry Jewish women? Go away!

MAN. And so he went.

NEVELSON. I told him I think I'd admire you better dead than alive.

MAN. O...K...So; you came back to America, after Hofmann threw you out.

NEVELSON. Yes, I came back for a while – to see Mike, in Maine, to make sure he was O.K.

MAN. Right.

NEVELSON. But before I came back I had another – what do you call it? – revelation.

MAN. One on top of the other!

NEVELSON. I jump around. Before I came back I was in Paris, and there was this thing called the Musee de L'homme...*(out)* this museum of so-called primitive art. It changed my life as much as Picasso did, and it changed *his* life, too.

MAN. *(out)* It was a museum of African sculpture. Picasso and Braque saw it when it opened, in nineteen oh nine.

NEVELSON. *(in)* Yes; way back. The meeting: think of it! Cubism and the so-called primitive. *(out)* It knocked Picasso out, and it knocked me out, too. This was before I went to Mexico – way before – before I saw the Mayan and the Aztec temples. Primitive!? That museum had some of the most sophisticated and powerful art I'd ever see. Picasso's cubism and this so-called primitive art. These two things; *they* changed me, too.

MAN. It's interesting that none of that African work was made as art.

NEVELSON. *(in)* Yes!

MAN. That it was all utilitarian.

NEVELSON. *(indicating)* Tell them what that means.

MAN. Uh…*(out)* Do you need this? That it was all useful?, made to be used? The masks were made to be worn in dance ceremonies?

NEVELSON. *(out)* Not just stuck on a wall to be looked at.

MAN. *(in)* Yes. *(out)* Nobody said "Hey, we're making *art.*" They were making things to be used as part of everyday life.

NEVELSON. *(still out)* It knocked me out. Things knock you out. Nobody in Africa'd studied with Hans Hofmann; nobody'd been to a museum; nobody'd ever heard the word "art," and there it was: pure power; pure art! I tell you!

MAN. *(in)* So, what did it *do* to you…to *your* stuff?

NEVELSON. *(in)* Not much; not right away; not for a long time. I'm slow; things get in there and work their way back up. *(out)* Do you know how long it took me from the time I came back from Europe that first time to the time I really felt – what!? – fulfilled? No! To when I said to myself, "You've done it! You've done it! You've become Louise Nevelson!

MAN. How long?

NEVELSON. *(in; slowly)* Twenty seven years!

MAN. That's a long time in the wilderness.

NEVELSON. Ahhh, wilderness came and went. Some times were bad, some times were O.K., but twenty seven years 'till I knew I'd done it. Twenty seven years.

MAN. Well, then, that's a lot of self-confidence.

NEVELSON. Self-confidence!? Four times I tried to kill myself, or I thought about it – wished I *could.* I lived off my family; Mike sent me money. Self-confidence!?

MAN. How'd you keep on going?

NEVELSON. I didn't know any better. *(out)* No, that's not right. This is what I know: you're an immigrant Jew; you're raised in a family scrapes its way up from poverty to...respectability and eventually even some... affluence; you're raised with these values; you marry *up*; you marry into a wealthy, uppercrust Jewish world. Forget it collapses when the market goes bust; forget that you've married into a world and that's one more thing, one more thing you take on and it falls apart – your whole world – the whole thing you were supposed to – what – *agree* to, become a part of? And it's all about the damn specialness you've felt about yourself ever since you were a little girl. You're special; you're talented; you're going to be somebody.

MAN. *Be* somebody?

NEVELSON. *(in)* Your*self*! Be your special *self*! O.K?

MAN. O.K.

NEVELSON. *(out)* You've known this from the beginning; you're very special; you're going to *be* somebody. No! You're going to be your*self*. You're going to find out who that "you" is – what that "you" is and you're going to...*occupy* that *space*...if it kills you.

MAN. And it almost does?

NEVELSON. *(in; softly)* Damn close. *(out)* I was humiliated. They raised me to be...to be – what? – self-reliant, and here I was practically begging them for food. And the whole marriage – arranged, or whatever? – what did I do to that!?

MAN. *(gentle)* What you had to.

NEVELSON. *(in)* Yeah, what turned out to be what I *had* to – not that I knew it while I was doing it. That was just… thrashing; thrashing around! *(out)* And so there it all was, special Louise, not so special Leah, really screwed up, ruined her marriage, living in New York City – hand to mouth – pretending to be an artist.

MAN. Weren't you working? I mean…making stuff?

NEVELSON. *(in)* Yeah; sure; and I even had stuff in shows, now and again: drawings, pottery, small…sculptural pieces, in places nobody ever heard of or went to, and nobody ever bought anything. And even when I had a show somebody came to see, you know what the critics said?

MAN. Yes.

NEVELSON. Yes? *(indicating audience)* Tell 'em!

MAN. *(out)* I quote: "We learned the artist is a woman in time to check our enthusiasm…"

NEVELSON. *(almost under her breath)* Son of a bitch.

MAN. "Had it been otherwise we might have hailed these sculptural expressions as by surely a great figure among moderns."

NEVELSON. Can you imagine? *(out)* I'd only put my last name on the pieces…Nevelson, but he found out.

MAN. *(in)* Well, there were a couple of good reviews, too…a couple of not bad ones.

NEVELSON. *(in)* It's only the rotten ones stick with you.

MAN. How true.

NEVELSON. *(out)* This show was at Nierendorf – a good gallery, and he took a chance on me. I'd gone into his gallery one day – cold! – and I said, "Mister Nierendorf, I want an exhibition in your gallery." And he said, "But I don't know your work; I don't know who you are." And I said, "Well, you can come and see my work." And he did; he came to where I was living and he looked at the work very thoughtfully, and then he said, very quietly, "You can have a show in three weeks."

MAN. You think somebody had cancelled?

NEVELSON. *(in)* Never look a gift horse in the mouth.

MAN. Even a big black one?

NEVELSON. Very funny. *(out)* "You can have a show in three weeks." He took a chance on me; it was the first time he'd ever shown an American artist.

MAN. Well, that was something.

NEVELSON. *(in)* Sure. Big deal. He sold...nothing. *(out)* He gave me another show a year later and then he died. Nobody bought anything.

MAN. But your family knew you were having shows.

NEVELSON. You know what somebody in the Nevelson family said? They said she probably pays for the shows – how was I supposed to do *that*!? I could barely get *food*! – or maybe she – you know – maybe she gives, what do they call them? "special favors"?

MAN. That's not nice.

NEVELSON. Tell me!

MAN. You *did* have it rough.

NEVELSON. I was a woman! I had another show – I don't remember where – paintings and little sculptural pieces, and nobody even mentioned I wasn't a man, and still nothing sold. Nobody bought a fucking thing? And they sent it all back to me – all of it – and what was I going to do?...So I took all they'd sent back and a hundred more paintings I had, and I took them off the stretchers and I *burned* them, and I destroyed the sculptures, too, and I gave all my tools to Mike, all my sculptural tools. Maybe he could use them, I thought. It wasn't a good time; it was a long, bad time.

MAN. Did you ever think maybe you were no good?

NEVELSON. *(pause; in)* I don't remember. No, I don't think I ever thought that, but I did think I'd maybe never get where I knew I could – to that space I knew I was supposed to stand in.

MAN. Occupy.

NEVELSON. Hm? Yeah; occupy. I met a nice guy, though –
during that show, a really nice guy.

MAN. Was it love?

NEVELSON. Well, a love affair; went on awhile.

MAN. But was it love? They tell me you frightened a lot of
men. They thought they wouldn't be up to you.

NEVELSON. Yeah?

MAN. Sure; you were big and gorgeous and crazy, and...

NEVELSON. Well, maybe most of them weren't up to me,
but I've met a few in my time I've...well, let me put it
this way: I'm not Emily Dickinson.

MAN. But I was talking about love.

NEVELSON. *(pause)* You learn after a while that there isn't
room for everything.

MAN. Pity.

NEVELSON. And, if you're any good you learn the difference between alone and lonely.

MAN. You've never been lonely?

NEVELSON. Sure; I was a *lot,* before I figured out who I was.

MAN. *(pinning it down)* Not since.

NEVELSON. As I said: there isn't room for everything. I've
had lots of men, lots of love affairs...well, some. All
interesting people.

MAN. Including some art dealers?

NEVELSON. I'd had enough of fat, bald men. I liked real
men, maybe a little younger than me, *real...men.* You
learn a lot about sex being a dancer. Did you know I
studied dance for over ten years?

MAN. Yes; I knew. Martha Graham?

NEVELSON. I knew her; I watched her. I didn't study there.
Of course you knew I did all that. You know a lot about
me.

MAN. And some of it's even true.

NEVELSON. *(out) (after gesturing him off)* You learn a lot about
your body, what it's capable of, what it needs...from

dance. Sex is good! It's healthy. It's healthy, and it's
nourishing. *(in)* I really did; I thought sex was great –
in its place, when it was needed, when it was…useful.

MAN. *(smiles)* Like so much else.

NEVELSON. *(tough agreement)* Yes; like so much else.

MAN. You never wanted another child?

NEVELSON. No! I screwed up once, and then there wasn't
room for it.

MAN. Meaning…?

NEVELSON. *(out)* How many times do I have to tell him!?
(in) Meaning, I didn't know who I was yet, so there's no
hand for anybody to take hold of. And when I *knew*…it
was too late…or I was too set.

MAN. You're tough.

NEVELSON. *(pause)* You're damn right.

MAN. A survivor.

NEVELSON. Nobody's going to do it for you. There were
really bad times – aside from the work, the…the stuff
that hurt. There was broke, as I told you, and humili-
ation and…do you know how tough it was to be an
artist and a woman?

MAN. You've told me.

NEVELSON. I know I've told you!

MAN. Even today. *(out)* Even today women have a harder
time than men – sales prices half men's, nowhere near
as many museum shows? Grudging acceptance?

NEVELSON. *(out)* The weaker sex; bullshit! You're not weak
if you can survive all that. But it was tough. We made a
group of Women Artists, and we showed together, and
that just made it worse. Solidarity? Hunh!

MAN. Yes. I mean no.

NEVELSON. Make up your mind. *(out; sudden choking up)*
And then my mother died!

MAN. *(sober)* Yes.

NEVELSON. I almost didn't get through *that* one. I think I
went to bed for six months. The poor woman!

MAN. *(genuine)* It's nice she was able to leave you a little money.

NEVELSON. *(in)* Yes; yes, it was. *(out)* Enough to buy a little place of my own, so I didn't have to live in those holes anymore. She knew; she understood. I rented half of it out...

MAN. To Peggy Guggenheim.

NEVELSON. *(in)* Yes *(out)* and I kept the rest as a studio and a place for Mike to come if he wanted.

MAN. Did he? Much?

NEVELSON. No; not too much; some. *(eager for a new subject)* And so, as I told you, it was a long time!

MAN. *(almost not believing)* Twenty seven years?

NEVELSON. Well, until the real breakthrough. Before that there was some progress, through all the bad stuff. But the first twenty years were really tough.

MAN. Twenty years – according to all the reports – of drinking and sleeping around and lying and conniving and...

NEVELSON. *(out; to cover him)* ...and painting and drawing and making pieces and keeping my eyes open – especially the ones in the back of my head...

MAN. ....and meeting all the wonderful people – the ones who were doing all the same things you were.

NEVELSON. Yeah, and some of them came through, got through it; some of them made it.

MAN. It was tough for *most* of you.

NEVELSON. *(in)* More for some. Now listen: about the drinking...

MAN. *(false surprise)* Drinking? What drinking?

NEVELSON. Cut it out. We Jews don't drink like other people; *you* know that. *(out)* But then I'm not *like* other people – other Jews, other *any*body. I used to sit around with the alkies sometimes, and I'd watch and I'd listen, and they had a kind of camaraderie, a whole world that made sense to them. They didn't seem lonely, and I was so lonely sometimes I'd make friends with a rat. But I wasn't a drunk; you have to understand that. *(in)* Sometimes…sometimes, if you're pushing yourself real hard, if your mind's spinning, you just have to…relax. Sometimes you just have to… go lie down.

MAN. For a week, maybe.

NEVELSON. *(thinks about it)* Maybe. Yeah, maybe a week and then you're all rested and you can go on.

MAN. Makes sense.

NEVELSON. *(some surprise)* Really?

MAN. Well; for you, sure.

NEVELSON. And then I got sick.

MAN. Oh?

NEVELSON. I had to have an operation. *(modest; points)*… down there.

MAN. The cervix?

NEVELSON. It was a tumor; women get them; it was fine.

MAN. A hysterectomy.

NEVELSON. Yeah; funny word for it. I wasn't hysterical; I was concerned, maybe. They cut it all out. They cut my past out. *(laughs glumly)*

MAN. *(genuine)* Gee.

NEVELSON. *(sighs)* Well, it let me concentrate more – on what was important.

MAN. The breakthrough; get to the breakthrough.

NEVELSON. *(sighs again)* O.K. *(out)* This is a lecture. *(in)* Do you want to…

MAN. No; I want to hear everything – especially this.

NEVELSON. *(shrugs)* O.K. *(afterthought)* You're sure!

MAN. Yes!

NEVELSON. O.K. *(out)* O.K. I want to talk to you about wood. I was wandering around one day and I saw some wood lying in the street – discarded stuff – and I said that looks nice and so I carted it home and put it in my studio. And then I did it the next day; oh, that looks nice, and so I took it home. And I had people *help* me. We'd go out for a walk and find wood – broken chairs, banisters, flat pieces, anything – and I'd collect it. I'd worked with wood before. I mean, I'd made sculpture out of wood and ceramic and all, but this was something else. I filled my house with it! My studio! My living area! Mike's room! My kitchen! The hallways! Everywhere! Finally it was floor to ceiling…piled up, everywhere! I moved the furniture out so I could have wood…I knew I was going to do *some*thing with it, but I didn't know *what*. And finally I did. What is all this good wood doing lying around my house in piles? Why is it *lying* there? Why don't I…and suddenly I knew! Stand it up! Make it all vertical! And it began to happen. *(Wood sculpture starts to appear.)* Small at first, and then bigger. *(More sculpture is revealed.)* And then I got the idea of stacking up wooden boxes and putting wood inside *them. (We see more.)* And suddenly there it all was! *(We see it.)* And it was wonderful! It was a whole world! And I looked at it and I started to dance. *(She does.)* And I danced, and I danced. I never felt more free in my life! *(stops; points)* There it was! My world! And I went on. *(We see more.)* Black; black; and then I did white, and then I did gold…And there it was. *(pointing)* There it all was. *(The stage is now filled with her work.)* All of a sudden I had become *me,* and I was *that!* *(points)* End of lecture. *(If audience applauds, handle it.)*

*(***MAN*** applauds, slowly, nodding) (in)* Thank you; thank you.

MAN. Just like that.

NEVELSON. Well, no; not just like that. It took a few years, but it was better and better, *(out)* and people looked and I had show after show and everything sold, and museums gave me whole *rooms* to fill, and…*(quieter)* and I became very famous…and I stayed that way… *(looks at walls)* Look at this, look at this…world. Isn't… that *some*thing? *(if audience applauds)* Thank you; thank you.

MAN. And all the bad years were over, and all the stuff you went through was...

NEVELSON. *(in)* Never forgotten! You never forget all that – and a lot you never forgive. *(out)* But if you finally come *into* yourself like I did, if you finally know the space you...occupy...well, then...you go on. You don't relax; you don't...bask in it. Now they want you; you're famous and they're throwing around words like great and magnificent, and so you go right *on*. You work harder than ever. You turn the world into one huge Nevelson. It was...fucking...wonderful. *(in)* And what was wonderful was what I'd always known would happen – deep inside of me – if I could only ever find it, if I could only hang on.

MAN. *(sincere)* I'm glad you did.

NEVELSON. *(chuckles)* Yeah; me too. And I outlived just about everybody – except Mike.

MAN. And how did he feel about it all?

NEVELSON. I don't want to go into it.

MAN. But...

NEVELSON. *(determined)* I said, I don't want to go into it! It was...complicated! He and I had problems; I...I don't want to go *into* it! He was *happy* for me! *Leave* it!

MAN. Well, he surely must have been happy you left him your entire estate.

NEVELSON. *(cold)* Yeah; well, it probably made up for a lot. You do what you can. Let's get off this!

MAN. *(grudging)* O...K.

NEVELSON. And so.

MAN. And so?

NEVELSON. *(cheerful again)* And so I became...well, I became a celebrity, on top of it all.

MAN. That surprised you?

NEVELSON. Hm?

MAN. You didn't work at it?

NEVELSON. Listen, dear: I learned: you use everything you can. If I was at the opening of one of my shows, I'd dress up really fine, so people would know I was there.

MAN. So people couldn't *not* notice you were there.

NEVELSON. Look! There's *Nevelson!* There's the *artist!* There she *is!*

MAN. Never hurts, I suppose.

NEVELSON. I told you before: I wasn't Emily Dickinson.

MAN. That was about sex.

NEVELSON. That was about everything.

MAN. A lot of people thought you were overdoing it.

NEVELSON. Sour grapes.

MAN. What did you *need?* You had fame; you had money. What did you need – friends?

NEVELSON. *(pause)* No; not really.

MAN. Love?

NEVELSON. *(pause)* No; not really.

MAN. What did you need then?

NEVELSON. *(pause)* Wood.

MAN. *(pause)* Yes. *(new tone)* You were famous for a long time.

NEVELSON. Yes.

MAN. And it was a great ride?

NEVELSON. A lot of it.

MAN. Not all?

NEVELSON. Once you get known the vipers come out from under the rocks – if that's where vipers come out from under.

MAN. I don't know; probably; sounds good.

NEVELSON. No matter. Dealers you've had shows with deep in the past claim contracts they've never had, or hold on to work after you've left them? There are lawsuits; there are claims made. And the envy starts: *(out)* "Oh, her assistants make all her work. She can't do it herself – a woman, and drunk all the time. And you know she never pays for her fancy clothes. She...forgets." Shit like that. *(in)* And no matter how it's going there are always a few knocks. The Met leaves you out of a show of the big U.S. artists. A couple of powerful critics never let you in the club, and the more you do – especially if you try to do something a little new – the more the carping starts: the shit!

MAN. You made a lot of enemies along the way.

NEVELSON. And a lot of new ones once I got there, but I finally got a good dealer – a young guy just starting out. Tough; bright; shrewd – and honest! *(out)* We made a good deal; he always paid me what he owed me; he advanced me money when I needed it – and then I didn't need it anymore – the advances.

MAN. He made you rich.

NEVELSON. *(in)* No; *I* made me rich.

MAN. Touche! *(beat)* O.K. What else?

NEVELSON. You tell me. What else?

MAN. Were the depressions all gone? And did the weeklong "lie downs" ever stop? The drinking?

NEVELSON. Not on your life! Something would always come up, throw a monkeywrench in there. I guess I didn't change all that much when things got better; it just became more...tolerable. And there was death to think about – dying.

MAN. I didn't know that ever worried you.

NEVELSON. No, but you get into your eighties you think about it more.

MAN. Still...what a ride!

NEVELSON. *(out) (laughs)* One lady informed me once – what, a few years before I died? – she was a journalist – we'd been talking about stuff I collected – this big collection of American Indian bowls and robes I had, and she'd read somewhere that I'd said that if I was reincarnated – not that I believed in that stuff – that if I was reincarnated I wanted to come back as an American Indian – because I loved everything American

Indian. So, she asked me if I still felt the same way. She asked me what I wanted to come back as. *(in)* And you know what I said?

MAN. No.

NEVELSON. I said I wanted to come back as Louise Nevelson.

MAN. A much better idea.

NEVELSON. *(sober) (in)* Is that a comfort?

MAN. Isn't it?

NEVELSON. I suppose. *(pause)*

MAN. Eventually you got very sick.

NEVELSON. Yeah, I sure did. *(out)* I smoked! I smoked a lot! I smoked all the time!

MAN. Thanks for not smoking now.

NEVELSON. *(in)* Do the dead smoke? Do the dead have cigarettes? Is the cigarette lobby that big!? *(out)* All the time – whenever I was conscious I had a cigarette in my mouth. They showed me an album once, pictures of me and there wasn't one I didn't have a cigarette in my mouth. Don't smoke! *(in)* Yeah; lung cancer.

MAN. Which they removed, gave you radiation, said it was all better.

NEVELSON. Yeah, and it was – for awhile, and then the headaches started. *(out)* It had… *(in)* What is the word?

MAN. Metastasized.

NEVELSON. Yes; that. *(out)* It had come back, and this time in my head. I went downhill pretty quick.

MAN. You were eighty-eight!

NEVELSON. Still!

MAN. *(laughs)* I heard a funny story!

NEVELSON. Well; cheer me *up*.

MAN. It's that when you were in the hospital for the last time, someone came to visit you and said she didn't even have to ask where your room was – that everybody in the hospital knew?

NEVELSON. I remember.

MAN. And that she came to your room and there was your name on the door as big as life...Louise Nevelson, in capital letters?

NEVELSON. As big as *death* maybe. Yes; I remember.

MAN. And that you had them take your name off the door...?

NEVELSON. Yes; there's no privacy anywhere.

MAN. And what did you have put up there instead?

NEVELSON. *(smiles)* Occupant.

MAN. *(smiles)* Yes; occupant...*(pause)* So; you died. They say you fought it, you fought it real hard.

NEVELSON. The pain was terrible. *(out)* But it always is in losing battles.

MAN. You were cremated.

NEVELSON. Sure. If they'd buried me someone would have probably put up some sculpture or something I would have hated.

MAN. And there's a rumor that when you died your nurse tied your big toes together – some primitive ritual?

NEVELSON. *(disbelief)* Noooooo! *(out)* So *what!* So my soul wouldn't sneak out from between my legs!? *(in)* People will say anything. Do you believe that?

MAN. Search me.

NEVELSON. *(to herself; snorting)* Tied my big *toes* together!

MAN. They gave you a big memorial service at the Metropolitan Museum.

NEVELSON. *(pleased)* Did they!

MAN. There were two hundred and fifty people there, and a lot of your friends spoke.

NEVELSON. I wish I'd been there!

MAN. *(pause)* So. It was a good life?

NEVELSON. *(considers)* Some; parts of it; enough; yes: enough.

MAN. *(points to sculpture)* You'd better go up there – occupy your space.

NEVELSON. Are we finished?

MAN. Just about. *(She crosses.) (out)* Ladies and Gentlemen…
the great American sculptor…Louise Nevelson.

End

Other Samuel French Publications by
Edward Albee...

All Over

A Delicate Balance

Breinigsville, PA USA
31 December 2009
230017BV00004B/1/P